D1249986

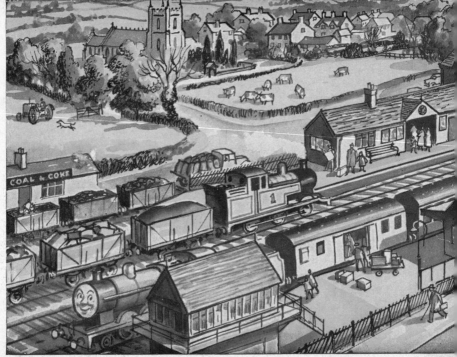

Railway Series, No. 18

STEPNEY
THE "BLUEBELL" ENGINE

by

THE REV. W. AWDRY

with illustrations by

GUNVOR & PETER EDWARDS

KAYE & WARD LIMITED
21 NEW STREET, LONDON EC2M 4NT

First published in volume form by
Edmund Ward (Publishers) Ltd 1963
Reprinted by Kaye & Ward Ltd
21 New Street, London EC2M 4NT
1967, 1971, 1975
First printed in paperback form 1971
Reprinted 1975

ISBN 0 7182 0017 9 *(hardback)*
ISBN 0 7182 0423 9 *(paperback)*

Printed in Great Britain by Tinling (1973) Limited, Prescot, Merseyside
A member of the Oxley Printing Group

Foreword

DEAR READERS,

Percy is a kind-hearted little engine. He feels sad because many fine steam engines are cut up on the Other Railway (B.R.)

Percy's ideas, however, though natural for an engine, are a little muddled. British Railways Officials are *not* cruel. They are sad to lose faithful steam friends, and glad to help engines to go to places like the Bluebell Railway at Sheffield Park in Sussex, where they can be cared for, and useful, and safe.

THE AUTHOR

. The author gratefully acknowledges the help given by fellow members of the Bluebell Railway Preservation Society, in the preparation of this book.

Bluebells of England

"The Bluebells are coming! Oho! Oho!
The Bluebells are coming! Oho! . . ."

"IF ye must sing, Percy," grumbled Douglas, "can't ye sing in tune? Anyway our song's aboot Campbells."

"And mine's about Bluebells."

"Then it's daft. Bluebells are flowers. Flowers can't come. They grow."

"My song isn't daft." Percy was indignant.

"It is then. I ken fine aboot bluebells. We've a song called 'The Bluebells of Scotland'."

"But," said Percy triumphantly, " 'The Bluebells of England' are different. They're engines, and one of them's coming with his Controller.

"Didn't you listen," he went on severely, "to the Fat Controller telling us about it?"

"I was away."

"Oh dear! I couldn't understand it all; but engines on the Other Railway aren't safe now. Their Controllers are cruel. They don't like engines any more. They put them on cold damp sidings, and then," Percy nearly sobbed, "they . . . they c-c-cut them up."

"Ye're right there," agreed Douglas. "If I hadn't escaped, I'd have been cut up too. It's all because of yon Diesels. They're all devils," he added fiercely.

"Fair play, Douglas," reminded Percy. "Some are nice. Look at Rusty and Daisy."

"Maybe so," answered Douglas, "I'd never trust one myself. But what I cannot understand is all your blether aboot bluebells."

" 'The Bluebells' are kind people who want to save engines. They've made a place in England called 'The Bluebell Railway'. Engines can escape there and be safe. . . ."

"Like me winning away here?"

"Yes," Percy went on, "just like that. If they are old or ill, a Fitter makes them well. They can have their own special colours, all the coal and water they need, and pull trains too."

"That's braw hearing," said Douglas with feeling.

"The Fat Controller says Stepney was the first engine to escape there, so he's asked him to visit us and bring his Controller."

"But," objected Douglas, "how aboot yon Diesels? Mightn't they catch him on the way?"

"We thought so too," said Percy, "but the Fat Controller says there's no danger of that. Stepney's a match for any Diesel. Besides, his Controller will take care of him."

"He's a brave engine for all that," said Douglas admiringly. "Fancy fighting his way through all those Diesels just to see us."

"Look!" squeaked Percy. "The Station's crowded."

"Silly! How can I look? Unless I'd be a cork-screw."

"Why've they all come? There's no train."

But Percy was wrong. The signal dropped, and from far away an engine whistled.

A gleam of yellow shone through the bridge girders. "Here he comes!" yelled Douglas.

"Poop! Poop! Peep! Peep!" the two engines whistled excitedly in welcome.

"Peeeep! Peeeeep!" replied Stepney, as with passengers and people waving and cheering, he puffed proudly through the Junction on the last stage of his long journey.

12

Stepney's Special

". . . So I tried very hard, but I couldn't work properly, and they put me on a siding. I stayed there for days and days. Other engines were there too. I was afraid. . . ."

"I'd have been frightened too," said Edward.

"But then, some workmen came. They mended me and even gave me a coat of paint. I couldn't understand it till my Driver came. He was very pleased. 'Stepney, you lucky old engine,' he said, 'you've been saved! The Bluebell Railway has bought you!'"

"What a lovely surprise," smiled Edward.

"Have they saved other engines besides you?" he asked.

"Oh yes," answered Stepney. "You'd like our Bluebell and Primrose. They're twins," he chuckled, "and as like as two peas. They only had numbers at first, Bluebell is 323 and Primrose is 27. They were very pleased when our Controller gave them names. Some say he was wrong to do it. It's certainly made them cocky, but they do work hard, and I think our Controller was right. *All* engines ought to have names."

"Yes," agreed Edward, "it's *most* important."

"That's why," Stepney continued, "we've given names to our 488 and 2650. But our Controller doesn't know. It's a secret. Don't tell him, will you?"

"Of course not," smiled Edward.

"They are both very pleased about it, because now they feel part of the family. We call 488 'Adams', after his designer, you know. He's a lovely engine, a South-Western from Devon. He can stroll away with any load he's given.

" 'Cromford', who's 2650, has been pulling trucks up high peaks in Derbyshire. He's tough is Cromford. He had to be for that job.

"Captain Baxter's tough, too," Stepney went on, "and rather rude. But he's worked in a Quarry, and you know what *that* does to an engine's language and manners."

"I do indeed," said Edward gravely.

"He's a good sort really," said Stepney. "I like him. We both miss our work with trucks."

He paused. "I oughtn't to say this," he went on, "after everyone's been so kind, but Our Line is very short, and I never get any good runs now. I miss them dreadfully."

"Never mind," smiled Edward. "Perhaps you'll get some while you're here."

Stepney said Goodbye to Edward and then returned to the Big Station. There he helped Duck shunt the Yard. They were soon great friends, and enjoyed their afternoon together.

Thomas arrived before they'd finished, and stayed till it was time for his last Branch Line train; but that train's tail lamps were hardly out of sight when the two engines heard a commotion at the Station.

"Hullo!" said Duck, "I wonder what's up."

Presently the night-duty Shunter came hurrying to the Shed . . . .

The bell in the Cabin on the Branch line rang once, then five, pause five. (That means shunt to allow following train to pass.) The Signalman was puzzled. He telephoned Control.

". . . A Special is it? . . . I see. . . ."

Thomas and his passengers grumbled at being delayed, but there was no help for it. Soon they heard an unfamiliar puffing, "Express" headlamps swayed and twinkled, then Stepney, pulling one coach, loomed in the Station lights. He slowed to exchange Tablets, whistled a greeting, then gathered speed into the night.

"Well! Bust my boiler!" said Thomas the Tank Engine.

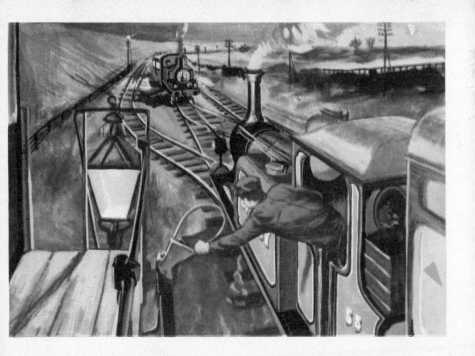

"Shunted!" fumed Thomas next morning. "On my own Branch too! It's a disgrace!"

"I'm sorry," said Stepney. "I was a Special," he explained.

"Why?"

"An important passenger came after you'd gone. He said he *must* get home, and ordered a Special. Duck kindly let me take it. We had a splendid run. No record-breaking, of course, but. . . ."

"Ah well," said Thomas modestly. "Perhaps when you know the road as I do. . . ."

"Exactly," put in Stepney. "You're such an expert." Thomas, flattered, forgot he was cross, and told Stepney all about his Branch Line.

Train Stops Play

"You are very lucky engines," said Stepney. "Your Branch has got everything. It's long enough to give you a good run, and you have plenty of passengers. Then you've a Quarry, a Mine and some Factories, so you need plenty of trucks. Trucks are fun," he went on wistfully, "I miss them on Our Line."

Percy looked surprised. "You can take mine and welcome, this morning," he said.

So they asked permission, and then went off to collect them. Toby and Thomas gaped in wonderment.

Stepney took his trucks to the Harbour, picked up a load of empties, and started back.

On the way they were stopped by a signal near a cricket field, where a match had just started. They settled down to watch.

Presently some fielders came towards them, and waved. "Could you move, please?" they asked. "Your last few trucks are behind the bowler's arm."

"Sorry," smiled the Driver. "Will this do?" and he eased Stepney forward till he stood under the signal.

The cricketers shouted their thanks, and play started again. The batsmen hit out, and soon a "skyer" towered towards the train.

Clunk—down went the signal.

There was another clunk, too, as the ball fell on the train, but neither Driver nor Fireman heard it. They were too busy.

"STOP!" yelled the fieldsmen; but Stepney's noisy starting drowned their shouts.

"Come along! Come along!" he puffed to the trucks, and left the frantic fieldsmen behind.

"Our one and only ball!" they said sadly.

Four of them piled into an ancient car. "Wake up, Caroline!" they said. Caroline coughed crossly, reluctantly came to life, and they rolled out on to the road.

Stepney wasn't hurrying. He had just crossed the river when Caroline came up behind.

"Tooooot! Tooooot!" she wailed.

Road and rail ran side by side. The cricketers waved and shouted, but they were too far away for the Fireman to recognize them or hear clearly what they said.

"If those jokers want a race," remarked the Driver, "they can have one." He advanced his Regulator, and Stepney drew ahead.

Poor Caroline wasn't happy. She rattled along at twice her usual speed. "Master shouldn't treat me like this," she grumbled. "This pace is too hot for my system. It'll fuse all my circuits.

"Hurrah!" she exclaimed. "That silly train has run into a hole, so we can't catch it. Now Master will have to be sensible and go home."

But Master didn't go home.

Caroline nearly boiled with fury when he made her climb a steep hill and run down to the Station on the other side.

Caroline arrived just as Stepney had shunted the trucks. His Crew were going off duty. The cricketers explained what had happened.

The Driver and Fireman were surprised. "Did you say the third truck from the Van?" they asked.

They all went and looked. The ball was there, nestling under some straw.

"We're very sorry," the Driver said.

"Never mind. You couldn't help it. Now we must get back quickly."

"That's just it," said the Driver. "You'll never be quick in Caroline. She looks worn out. . . . . Wait a minute," he went on. "I've got a plan."

The Driver spoke to the Stationmaster and Signalman. Then they rolled Caroline on to a flat truck, and coupled a Brakevan behind. The cricketers got in, and Stepney pulled the train. They reached the field in no time.

Stepney watched from a siding while Driver, Fireman and Guard sat in the Pavilion. There were no more lost balls, and the game was played to an exciting finish.

Even Caroline was pleased. She doesn't think trains silly now. "They have their uses," she says. "They can save the wear on a poor car's wheels."

Bowled Out

THE big Diesel surveyed the shed. "Not bad," he said. "I've seen worse. At least you are all clean."

The engines gaped.

"It's not your fault," he went on, "but you're all out of date. Your Controller should scrap you, and get engines like me. A fill of oil, a touch on the starter, and I'm off, with no bother, no waiting. They have to fuss round you for hours before you're ready."

At last the engines found their voices. An Inspector had to come and stop the noise!

They held an indignation meeting early next morning round the turntable.

"Disgraceful!" rumbled Gordon.

"Disgusting!" said James.

"Despicable!" spluttered Henry.

"To say such things to us!" burst out Donald and Douglas. "It's to teach him a lesson we'd be wanting."

But no one had any good ideas, and at last they all went off to work except for Duck and Stepney. "Never mind," said Duck. "We'll be sure to think of something."

"We'll have to be quick then," warned Stepney.

But their chance came sooner than expected.

Diesel purred comfortably. He was being warmed up well before time. An Inspector watched a Fitter making adjustments. The wind tugged at the Inspector's hat.

The Fitter replaced the air-intake cover. "O.K., mate," he said.

Diesel saw his coaches waiting at the platform. He rolled proudly towards them. "Look at me, Duck and Stepney," he purred. "Now I'll show you something." He advanced a few yards, then suddenly he coughed—faltered—choked—and stopped.

The Inspector meanwhile had seen nothing of this. He was looking for his hat.

"Can we help you at all?" asked Duck and Stepney sweetly. Diesel seethed with baffled fury as they pushed him back to the Shed.

"My hat!" exclaimed the Inspector, as the cavalcade went by.

"Bother your hat!" said the Fat Controller crossly. "The train's due out in ten minutes, and you'll have to take it, Duck."

Duck looked doubtful, but when Stepney asked, "Can I help him, Sir?" he felt better. The Fat Controller was pleased too, and hurried away almost cheerfully to make the arrangements.

The engines and their Crews made careful plans. "A good start's everything on a job like this," warned Stepney, so, as they backed down, they dropped sand on the rails, rolling it firm with their wheels.

Both Controllers were there to see them off. "Gordon will take over from half way," said the Fat Controller, "so get the train there. Never mind about being late. Good luck!"

"Don't worry, Sirs," smiled Stepney. "We'll get there, *and* be early too!"

They stood waiting, sizzling with excitement, ready and eager to be off.

At last the Guard's flag waved. The engines dug their wheels into the sand, and gave a mighty heave. "Come On! Come ON!" puffed Duck, while Stepney barked excitedly in front. Moving carefully over the points, they reached the open line.

"Now for a sprint," wuffed Stepney.

"I'm ready when you are," puffed Duck.

Faster and faster they went, till their wheels were turning at such speed that the side-rods were merely blurs. Under clear signals they whizzed through Edward's Station, and charged at Gordon's Hill beyond.

They felt the drag of their fifteen coaches here. It was hard work, but once over the top the last ten miles were plain running, and they swept into the Big Station in fine style.

"Hullo!" said Gordon. "You're early. That's one in the headlamp for old Diesel! Have you heard the latest?" he chuckled. "Diesel had sucked the Inspector's hat into his air-pipe. That's why he broke down. James says he's sick as boiler sludge, and sulking in the Shed. Out of date are we? Ho! Ho! Ho!" and still laughing, Gordon puffed away.

Everyone was sad next day when Stepney had to go. All the engines who could, came to see him off. The Fat Controller made a speech, and so did Stepney's Controller.

Donald and Douglas made everyone sing "Auld Lang Syne", and then Stepney and his Controller puffed off to a chorus of cheers and whistles.

"Goodbye, Stepney. Come again, Goodbye, Goodbye."

But what about Diesel? He'd slipped away the night before. He said Goodbye to no one, but left two things behind: the nasty smell of bad manners, and a battered bowler hat!